When Theresa Tomlinson was young she wanted to be a dancer – not a writer at all. It wasn't until she gave up teaching to become a full-time mother that she began to write stories to entertain her three children, taking inspiration from childhood memories of the North Yorkshire and Cleveland coast. Her first book was *The Flither Pickers*, and she has since written many other titles, including *Riding the Waves* (Commended for the 1991 Carnegie Medal), *Haunted House Blues* and the Time-Slip Adventures series: *Meet Me by the Steelmen*, *Night of the Red Devil* and *Scavenger Boy*. "I write full-time now," she says. "I love it." Theresa Tomlinson lives in Whitby with her architect husband and her cat, Mewsli.

For Florence May Casling Simpson

SCAVENGER BOY

THERESA TOMLINSON

illustrations by

ANTHONY LEWIS

WALKER
BOOKS

AUTHOR'S NOTE

Michael and his family are invented characters, though I would like to thank my nephew Michael Johnston for allowing me to use his name. Cromford Mill, near Matlock in Derbyshire, now has World Heritage Site status and is open to the public daily. Richard Arkwright and his mill worker John Thompson were both very real people. The author would like to thank Trisha Stamp and Martyn Gillie of the Arkwright Society for their kind help and advice, and also some of the children from Cromford Church of England Primary School, North Street, who read the manuscript with their teacher and gave encouraging feedback.

First published 2003 by Walker Books Ltd
87 Vauxhall Walk, London SE11 5HJ

2 4 6 8 10 9 7 5 3

Text © 2003 Theresa Tomlinson
Illustrations © 2003 Anthony Lewis

This book has been typeset in Plantin

Printed and bound in Great Britain by
Clays Ltd, St Ives plc

British Library Cataloguing in Publication Data:
a catalogue record for this book is
available from the British Library

ISBN 978-0-7445-5997-2

www.walker.co.uk

Contents

Chapter 1

Bits and Bobs

It was just a bit of old wood shaped like a
huge cotton reel. A crack ran right across the
top of it, so Michael couldn't believe the
price ticket – one pound. He'd got
exactly one pound in his pocket, but he'd
complained to his mother, "You can't get
anything worth having for a pound."

Michael stared down at the giant, cracked
cotton reel. It was a bit of old junk! Asking a
pound for it really took the biscuit! How dare
the woman stallholder offer such a thing for
sale?

A poster pinned on the front of the stall
said BITS AND BOBS. What was the cracked
reel supposed to be, a bit or a bob? It sat
there between hanks of wool, old chipped
plates and teacups.

Michael picked a short piece of cream-coloured thread off the reel and flicked it away. The smooth, waxy surface of the wood did feel rather nice to touch, and his hand fitted neatly round the stem of the reel, but then— The whole thing seemed to twitch just slightly, of its own accord, rather like those joke jumping beans that start to move when your hand warms them up. It gave him quite a shock and he put it down quickly.

"Cheer up, it might never happen!" the woman said.

Her jolly words made Michael feel worse. "It just did," he muttered and moved quickly on to the next stall, full of knitted dolls and tea-cosies and some more of those strange wooden reels. These ones were in better condition and they cost two pounds, but still Michael couldn't help thinking that they sold some very odd things in Cromford.

He wondered if he'd be better off leaving the market-place and going into the village shop; at least he'd be able to get a bar of chocolate for a pound.

Michael wandered on to the next stall, shoulders hunched, feeling cold and wishing that he'd got his new fleece. That fleece was folded away somewhere among the piles of packing cases that were being carried into the little house on North Street. They'd come to live in the small Derbyshire village of Cromford and Michael had been sent out of the house while his parents and the removal men were carrying things inside.

At first he'd tried to help, but the removal men were staggering under the weight of wardrobes and sideboards and his parents were both giving the men different instructions. Voices were getting sharper and sharper, and somehow Michael always seemed to be standing just where the heaviest pieces of furniture were about to be placed.

"I tell you what," said his mother, her hair standing on end as she fished frantically in the pocket of her jeans. "You take this pound and go and find something to buy in that little market we saw, just down the hill. Make sure you use the crossing by the traffic lights!"

"By myself?" Michael was amazed at the suggestion.

"Yes. Good idea," his dad said. "You can do things like that in a village. You should be safe just walking down the road and crossing over at the lights."

"Can't get anything for a pound," Michael groaned, but he took the coin and did as they suggested. It was no fun being in the house and just as cold inside as out, with the front door standing open and no heating on yet.

Michael wandered on through the market, past stalls of Christmas cards, homemade-looking sweets and more of those big wooden reels, in different shapes and sizes. Everything cost more than a pound.

He stopped at a stall that had terribly expensive teddy bears, but when the old woman stallholder started smiling at him he moved on quickly again. He didn't want to speak to anyone and he certainly didn't want anyone smiling at him. What he really wanted was to go back home to his big, comfortable house in Nottingham, with his cosy, familiar bedroom full of games and books.

Michael sighed. He knew that wasn't possible – there was no going back. His parents were both textile designers who'd run a small but successful studio in Nottingham, until last year, when their business had failed. The big company that usually bought their designs had gone bankrupt and all Mum and Dad's hard work had brought in no money.

They'd been very worried and miserable for a while, but then Mum had this bright idea. They'd sell the big Nottingham house and with the money they'd buy a smaller house, along with all the equipment they'd need to advertise new designs over the Internet.

"It wouldn't matter where we lived." Mum was bursting with excitement. "We could go and live in the countryside, in a village. That would be lovely for Michael!"

Michael hadn't been at all sure that it would be lovely; it sounded mad to him and very unsettling, but he was glad to see his parents smiling again.

"I've always loved those stone-built weavers' cottages that we saw in Cromford," Mum pleaded. "They're close to the Old Mill, where lots of people visit. We could probably sell our designs in the mill too."

"Mmm – textiles from Cromford?" Dad mused. "We could call ourselves 'Cyber-mill Designs'."

"'Crazy-mad Designs'," Michael muttered.

So that was how Michael came to be wandering round Cromford market-place on a cold November afternoon as it started to get dark. Suddenly he realized that the market stallholders had begun packing up. He looked over at the village shop, but the woman was just turning around the sign that said CLOSED. Why hadn't he gone earlier? He felt like growling!

Chapter 2

A Sign of Good Luck

At last he decided he'd better go back to North Street and save his pound. As he went past the BITS AND BOBS stall he saw the cracked reel still there. The woman who'd spoken to him was nowhere to be seen. He picked the reel up again.

"Is it a bit or a bob?" he muttered.

"Oh, I should say it's definitely a bob," a voice answered him, as the woman appeared from beneath the back of the stall where she'd been packing up her goods.

"A bob?" Michael was puzzled.

"Well – it's a bobbin. Of course you know what a bobbin is?"

He didn't really, but the bobbin rolled backwards and forwards in his hand, almost as though it had a life of its own.

"That's a very special thing round here,"

the woman went on. "The whole of Cromford once turned on bobbins. Bobbins and water – they're everywhere!"

Michael hadn't a clue what she was on about, but somehow the bobbin had begun to interest him and it was, after all, only a pound. "I'll have it," he said.

The woman put it into a brown paper bag for him. "You won't regret it," she said.

Michael took the package and carefully crossed the road, then wandered back up to North Street. He was relieved to see that the removal van had gone. As he walked up the street, his spirits rose; the little house looked better with its lights on and he found a fire was crackling in the grate.

"Oh good," said his dad. "You're back. Just in time for fish and chips. We've got the table and chairs, but can't find the cutlery."

"We'll have to use our fingers," Michael was surprised to hear his mother say.

The fish and chips and the fire made him feel much better.

"D'you want to see what I got?" he asked as they sat there sipping hot cups of tea from polystyrene beakers. The tea had come from the fish and chip shop too, because they couldn't find the cups – or the tea bags, for that matter.

Both his parents looked very tired and dirty. His mother, usually so clean and smart, had two great smudges of dust on her cheeks.

His dad yawned and scratched his head. "So you did find something for a pound after all?"

"It wasn't easy," Michael told them. He picked up the brown paper package from beneath his chair and tipped the large cotton reel with its cracked top out onto the table, where it rolled for a moment, then stopped. Both his parents stared.

"It's a bobbin," Michael told them.

"Of course it is," his mother smiled. "I bet it's from one of the big spinning machines they used to have in the Old Mill. Fancy you buying that, Michael!" She shook her head, still surprised. "What a very interesting thing to buy."

Michael's father picked it up and let it roll across his hand. "Fancy you buying a bobbin instead of a bar of chocolate."

"It was a close thing," Michael admitted.

"You couldn't have bought anything more typical of Cromford." His mother's eyes were suddenly bright, almost as though she wanted to cry, and Michael was worried for a moment that he'd upset her. But she didn't cry; she smiled instead. "This must be a sign of good luck," she added. "We were right to come here."

Dad turned the bobbin upside down, then suddenly bent his head to look closely at the bottom. "Look here – somebody's carved their initials on it. Is it EL?"

Michael grabbed the bobbin and examined it himself. He could see two rough, sloping letters cut into the underside, where it wasn't cracked at all. "No, it's F," he said. "FL. It's not very clear though. Could be Fred! Could be Frank!"

He put the bobbin in the middle of the mantelpiece, relieved that at least they didn't think him mad for bringing back a cracked old thing like that.

His parents sat there beside the fire, yawning and rubbing their aching backs, talking quietly about what they should do the next day. There was still so much to sort out that they didn't know where to start, but they were talking happily together now and all the sharpness of the morning seemed to have faded.

"We should all get to bed," Mum insisted. Michael was so tired that he didn't argue, even though when he went upstairs he discovered that he had to bed down in a sleeping-bag with a cushion for his head, because the bedclothes couldn't be found either.

"I don't much like this little room," he complained as he climbed into the sleeping-bag. "It's cold and bare and there's no carpet or curtains."

"We'll paint it tomorrow, if you like. What colour would you want it to be?"

"Orange," he murmured. And despite the strange room and the lack of curtains, he soon fell asleep.

Chapter 3

As Though It Belongs

It was still dark when Michael woke in the morning and getting dressed was a cold business. He threw on the same clothes that he'd been wearing the day before and didn't bother much with washing, as the water in the taps seemed pretty cold too.

Breakfast was toast and chocolate spread, and for once neither of his parents seemed to complain about the great dollops that Michael was scooping out of the jar.

"Right," said Mum. "Let's get on with Michael's bedroom. Are you sure you want it to be orange?"

"Yes!" Michael was definite.

They drove into Matlock and came back with a large tin of bright orange paint. By the time it was lunch, he and his mother had already got one wall finished. His father carefully painted the windowsill white, then started on the ceiling. He scraped at one of the strong wooden beams up there. "Funny – that's funny," he said. "I'm sure…"

"What?" Michael asked.

"Another FL!"

"Let me see," Michael pleaded.

His father came down and held the ladder steady while Michael climbed up. He could see clearly where his father had lightly brushed orange paint over the letters FLO cut deep into the low roof beam. "Just like my bobbin," he said, "but it's got an O as well."

"That's what I thought," Dad laughed. "But it can't be."

Michael frowned. He rushed downstairs and reappeared almost at once, gasping for breath, with the bobbin in his hand. "It *is* the same," he insisted, struggling up the ladder. He held the bobbin beside the carved marks on the roof beam, his hand shaking a little. "See, it *is* the same! Look, the F is sloping backwards and the L is sloping the other way on them both. They're like the letters I used to do when I was small."

Both his parents peered at the marks. "Well," his dad said at last, "I've got to admit that's peculiar. It's almost as though that bobbin belongs here in this house."

"I think it does," said Michael. Though he really couldn't explain why or how.

Later that night, while the paint was drying, they went for a stroll around the village. They walked through the little market-place, and behind the Greyhound Hotel they found a great pond of water with a waterwheel at one end. Ducks paddled around the edges and the reflected lights from the cottage windows gleamed on the water. "Water everywhere!" Dad said.

"Bobbins and water!" Michael muttered. He was sure he'd heard that before, but he couldn't quite think where.

That night Michael's parents insisted that

he sleep downstairs on the couch while the paint in his bedroom dried properly. "You don't want to be breathing in those fumes, and it'll be nice and warm by the fire," said his mother.

"And you need a good night's sleep, ready for school in the morning," Dad added.

Michael's heart sank at those words. He dreaded the thought of going off to the village school that stood at the top of North Street. Though he hadn't really wanted to come to Cromford, he'd begun to enjoy the painting and sorting out that they'd been doing. He now felt that he'd much rather stay in the little house with his parents than go off to a strange school where nobody knew him.

But Michael was very tired and the fire warm and comforting, so he soon drifted off to sleep. It was only when he woke in the morning and remembered he had to go to school that his stomach tied itself into a knot again. He refused to eat any breakfast.

"But you must," his mother begged.

"I can't!" said Michael. "I feel sick. I'm too ill to go to school – got bellyache. I'll stay here and help you get the work-room ready."

"No," his father was firm. "We've got the website designer coming and a lot to do. You'll feel better once you've been. Get your coat and I'll walk up with you and speak to the headteacher."

Michael knew that tone of voice. He wasn't going to get out of this, but he felt terrible. He went to stand in front of the warm fire, turning his back on his parents. "Get it yourself!" he growled.

There was a tense silence and Michael feared that his dad would start to shout, but instead his mother came over and gave him a hug.

"It'll be all right," she soothed, stroking his shoulder. Then she picked up the bobbin from the mantelpiece. "Why don't you take this along and show it to your teacher? It'll be something to talk about, help get you settled in."

Michael shrugged his shoulders. It didn't seem like much of an idea to him, but once again the warm, smooth bobbin in his hand felt good. A touch of warmth seemed to creep up his arm and into his chest and stomach, soothing away the horrible knot of worry. He supposed he could take it along. What was there to lose?

"OK," he agreed.

He turned around and there was his father, patiently holding out his coat for him to put on.

Chapter 4

A Little Piece of History

Michael's teacher, Mr Price, was a young man who looked as though he was barely out of school himself.

"This is my first term here too," he told Michael. "I've only been here six weeks myself." Then almost at once he swooped down on the bobbin that Michael still clutched in his hand. "Ah – now that's brilliant!" he said. "That's a wonderful little piece of history, that is! I'm planning a project on Arkwright's Mill later in the term." He took the bobbin and held it up to show the rest of the class.

Michael thought they looked unimpressed, except for one girl who wore glasses and sat near the front. She peered at the bottom of the bobbin where it said FL in a very interested way, but then Michael decided that she was probably just short-sighted.

Somehow Michael managed to get through the day. Everybody was friendly, but that didn't stop things being strange and different.

"I've got a bobbin like that at home," said one boy.

"So've I," said another. "Have you got any football cards?"

"Yes," Michael told them. "But they're still packed away."

"Do you want to do swaps? Bring them tomorrow!"

"I'll try." Michael wasn't at all sure he'd be able to find them.

Break seemed very different because the playground had grass in it instead of just tarmac. In Nottingham, the school playground was surrounded by high brick walls, with rows and rows of houses beyond them. Here you could see green and purple hills stretching for miles, divided up by grey stone walls and dark, craggy outcrops of rock. Sheep and cows wandered about looking for fresh grass.

He was exhausted when at last the buzzer went for hometime. He stood for a moment at the school gate, waiting vaguely for his mother to come and pick him up in the car, as she'd done every day in Nottingham. The girl with the glasses, whom he now knew as Sarah, pushed past him, looking at him a little strangely.

"Aren't you going home?" she asked.

Then quickly Michael realized how ridiculous he was being. He could see his house down at the bottom of North Street from the school gate. All he had to do was walk along the pavement and he'd be there.

"Course I am," he told her, grinning foolishly. He picked up his bag and set off, following her down the street. He saw that Sarah went into the end house, two doors down.

When he opened his own front door and went in, it was hard to believe it was the same box-piled house that he'd left that morning. The floor in the living-room was covered with their old carpet from Nottingham and the red curtains that went with it had been cut down to fit the smaller windows. Gleaming plates and cups were arranged on the dresser shelves and a smell of proper cooking drifted out from the kitchen.

"Hi," his mother called out from the top of the house. "We're up here! How's it gone?"

"OK," he told her as he strode upstairs. He found them in the big attic room, with the long row of weaver's windows that let in an amazing amount of light. They'd set up drawing boards and art materials in front of the windows and two computers, a scanner and a printer, in the darker end of the room. "Wow! You've done a lot," he told them.

"Yep! We haven't stopped," said Dad. "Our website's up and running. Do you want to see it?"

*　　*　　*

That night Michael was able to sleep in his newly painted bedroom. Thick velvet curtains were now drawn across his window, so that he slept deeply in peaceful darkness.

He went off to school by himself the following morning, without any anxiety, but when he got to school he found his classroom full of wooden bobbins. Mr Price was pink-faced with delight as he was presented with small bobbins, long bobbins, polished bobbins, cracked bobbins.

"Oh, Jennifer, that's wonderful! And another one – thank you, James!"

"My nan sent this one. Her mother brought it out from the mill when she worked there as a little lass!"

"My grandad has this un on his mantelpiece, Mr Price. He polished it up for his mam!"

Michael felt strangely disappointed. He realized that there was nothing very special about his old cracked bit of wood. It seemed that every house in Cromford possessed at least one bobbin.

As they worked through their maths and English exercises, Michael kept glancing at the bobbins piled high on the display table. "Can't even tell which is mine!" he murmured.

The pile of bobbins stayed there all week and Michael began to feel quite settled at his school. The days passed quickly. It was during the Friday afternoon that a rustle of excitement went through the whole class. "Snowing!" somebody whispered as the first big flakes went drifting past the classroom windows.

"Hurray! It's settling!"

"Snowball fight!" someone else called out.

Mr Price told them to get on with their work, but he smiled and added, "Snowball fight at hometime!"

"We'll get you, Priceless!" somebody whispered.

Mr Price chuckled and said, "We'll see!"

Even though the snow came on steadily,

turning the rooftops and playground walls white, Michael found himself distracted by the pile of bobbins still there on the display table. He couldn't tell which one was his. His must be right at the bottom somewhere. The thought kept coming into his mind that if there were so many other bobbins just like his – well, he might as well have his back again.

Chapter 5

Twist and Turn

When the buzzer went for the end of lessons, everyone dashed outside, hauling on their coats as they went, scarves flying; but Michael hung back, by the display table. He took a quick glance around to see that he was alone and started fishing about among the pile of bobbins. Some clattered onto the floor making him think Mr Price might come back, and he just didn't want to have to explain what he was doing. Then one of the bobbins was suddenly there in his hand, almost as though it had jumped into his grasp with a little twist and turn. He looked carefully and saw FL cut roughly into it.

"What're you up to?" It was Sarah watching him from the door.

He felt resentful. "It's mine." He waved the bobbin at her. "I can have it back if I want!"

"Yes, course you can," she agreed calmly. "I wouldn't bring my bobbin to school."

"Why?" he asked, surprised.

"My bobbin was my great-great-grandmother's treasure. It's supposed to bring our family luck. I'd never risk losing it by bringing it here. Well, put it in your schoolbag, if you want it back," she told him sensibly. "Keep it safe!"

He did as he was told.

Michael followed Sarah down North Street, but stopped suddenly halfway down, feeling that something was rustling around in his bag. He looked inside, but everything seemed still and normal. Then, as he reached for the bobbin, he felt sure that it gave another of those funny little twists in his hand.

"So you want to roll, do you?" he said, and he started rolling it vigorously backwards and forwards in his hand as he walked on. When he stopped outside his own front door a touch of panic grew inside his stomach.

He was holding his hand perfectly still now, but the bobbin was turning very slowly and steadily of its own accord.

He could even feel the waxy wood scraping against his skin, a strange and rather frightening sensation. It had no business to be turning like that. OK, he'd started rolling it, but a dead piece of wood just wasn't supposed to move unless you made it move.

Michael's stomach bunched itself up into a nasty knot again. He'd got to stop this; he'd got to get a grip. He grabbed the bobbin tightly round the wooden shaft that ran from top to bottom and for a moment he thought he'd succeeded, but then he gradually realized that something even worse was happening. The bobbin was still in his hand but now, with a dizzying, sickening lurch, he realized that he himself was slowly turning with it.

He dropped his schoolbag and grabbed the bobbin with both hands, but that only seemed to speed things up. He gritted his teeth and held on tight to the bobbin as his vision blurred and North Street spun around him.

"Help! Help!" he murmured weakly. He shut his eyes and hoped that his mother would come and wake him from what must surely be a dreadful dream, but then he began to feel that he was slowing down. He dared to open his eyes and felt reassured to see that North Street was swinging slowly round him.

Then at last he was standing still once again, though he felt a little giddy. It was still snowing. He couldn't see Sarah ahead of him, but it was definitely his own front door that he was standing in front of, so that was OK. Then he glanced back up to the top of the street and got the most tremendous shock, for where his school was supposed to be, he could see nothing but allotment gardens with goats and pigs, and the high grassy hillside.

Where had his school gone? He was just

getting used to it! That crazy twisting bobbin had somehow made it vanish. And where was the bobbin now? His hands were empty – both the bobbin and his bag had gone, along with the school.

Michael's heart was beating wildly. Something terrible had happened to him, but what? There was no time to work things out because he heard the sound of clopping feet behind him and turned to see a wooden cart pulled by a dusty black and white pony coming up North Street. Two men walked beside it, looking at the houses.

"This is it, number twenty," one of them said, pointing at Michael's front door.

The other grabbed the pony's harness. "Whoa!" he shouted and the pony stopped.

The cart was piled high with old furniture and children of all ages. Michael couldn't move or speak; his whole body and mind were frozen. All he could do was stand and watch as the tired-looking man who'd spoken first fished out a key from his pocket and went to turn it in the lock of the door – *his* door.

"Now what do you think, Ma?" He turned back to the cart, smiling.

A thin woman in a long worn skirt, with a faded shawl pulled tightly round her shoulders, clambered down from the cart, her mouth trembling. "I think it's a palace, Jethro," she said, her eyes swimming with tears.

"It *is* a palace, Ma!" the children shouted. "It's a palace true enough! And it's for us, Ma!"

The key turned in the lock and then the children came leaping down from the cart and rushed inside Michael's house. A girl, dressed like her mother in long skirt and shawl, gave him a curious look as she passed in front of him.

"They wear strange garb in Cromford," she muttered, looking him up and down from his hooded fleece to his grey, faded trainers.

Michael was so stunned and shocked that he just stood there with his mouth open. As the girl passed close to him, he wrinkled his nose; there was a very stale whiff about that girl. His mother would have insisted on a good bath and hair-wash if he'd smelt like that. But grubbiness didn't seem so very important when the real problem was that they were bursting into his house as if it were their own.

Michael could hear cries of delight.

"Ooh, Ma! Look at the whitewashed walls!"

"Ooh, Ma! *Ma!* Look at the shining black stove!"

Michael frowned. What were they on about? His parents had just painted the walls a strong green colour and there was certainly no black stove. What would his parents be thinking at this invasion? Michael hesitated for a moment, then he followed them inside. Well, after all, it was his house! But he got even more of a shock then, for his parents' cosy decoration had vanished. All the familiar furniture was gone and true enough, the walls were bare and whitewashed. His mother's favourite crockery had vanished too, but a great black shining stove stood there in the kitchen instead.

He realized then that everyone had gone very quiet, staring at him. "Is tha from the mill?" the father asked.

Michael shook his head. All he could think to say was, "I live here!"

Chapter 6

One Lodger's No Trouble

There was a moment of silence while the
family all continued to stare at Michael, but
then the woman suddenly nodded as though
she understood. "I see," she said, and came
and patted his shoulder. "I thought it were
too good to be true, Jethro – one family to a
whole house! I've never heard o' such a thing!
He's to lodge wi' us! In't that right?"

"Aye," the man nodded. "Course he is.
Tha's welcome to lodge wi' us lad!"

Though these people seemed friendly
enough, somewhere at the back of Michael's
head a very worrying explanation began to
grow. He'd seen pictures of women dressed
like this, and those pictures had been in
history books. He'd seen pictures of young
lads, just like those who stood about him,
wearing clumsy wooden clogs on their bare

feet – but those people in the pictures had lived a long time ago.

"Well," said the woman, kindly, "one lodger's no trouble to us. We can manage that all right, in a fine big house like this, can't we, Jethro?"

"Aye." The man nodded, just as friendly. "No trouble at all! My name is Jethro Barraclough, weaver o' Derby – that was, till today."

"I'm Michael, Michael from Nottingham," he murmured as Jethro shook his hand.

The weaver's hands were strong and leathery. "We'd be grateful for a bit o' help wi' the unloading," he said. "Then Ma will make a bit o' supper before the lads go off to do their night shift. Mr Arkwright has loaned us a day's wage to buy oats, so there'll be plenty o' porridge to spare."

Jethro fished in his pocket and brought out a piece of newspaper that had been carefully cut. He went to prop it up on the wooden mantelpiece that stood above the stove.

"There now," he said. "That's what brought us here, that little bit of paper, and I pray we've done right! Here we are and here we must stay. You can't fight progress! We've got to move with the times. They'll all work for such as Arkwright in the end."

Michael moved closer to read the little cutting, his hands and knees shaking as he saw the words, letters formed strangely, but quite readable.

WANTED
At Cromford, in the County of Derby,
Weavers, with large Families. Like wise
children of all ages: above seven Years old,
may have constant Employment.
September 19, 1781

Michael stared at the date – 1781. He'd begun to suspect something like this, but how could it have happened? It was definitely something to do with that crazy bobbin. It had somehow brought him here, twisting and turning and spinning the years backwards, and now it had left him here and vanished. How was he ever going to get back to his parents and their little Internet studio in the attic?

Suddenly he realized that the family were all staring curiously at him again. "He can read, Ma!" the girl whispered. "He can read those words that brought us here! Those words that the minister spelt out for us!"

The father suddenly laughed and clapped Michael on the shoulder. "Well, fancy us having a lodger that can read, Ma! Fancy that! No wonder he don't work at the mill. Now come on, all hands needed – we must get this cart unloaded."

All at once there was a great rush outside again. Jethro led the way, calling out orders, and even the smallest toddling child was soon carrying their possessions into the house: wooden stools, heavy iron pots and pans, a rocking chair and a big wooden tub. There was nothing else to do but try to help. The girl, who seemed to be about Michael's age, dumped a very smelly rolled-up strong cotton mattress into his arms.

"Where shall I take it?" he asked.

"Upstairs a'course. Tha's a bit slow for someone who can read," she said cheekily.

"Tek n'notice o' Flora," a boy said. "She's my twin. She's got a big mouth and a big bum! I'm George."

Flora dumped another smelly mattress into George's arms. "Shut up, our George, and get on," she said. "That bell will be ringing for night shift and tha'll have had nowt to eat."

That seemed to make George hurry up and he pushed past Michael and led the way upstairs. Michael wondered what he'd see as he struggled upstairs with the bedding. The walls were whitewashed and his little room didn't exist; there was just one large sleeping space, with a big wooden bed with sacking stretched over the sturdy frame. Six other small box beds lined the walls like a youth hostel dormitory. There was not a bit of space to spare.

"This is truly a palace!" George cried in delight. "Beds provided! No more will I sleep on the floor!"

Michael was amazed: it was a tiny house for so many people, with no warm radiators and cold, bare floorboards! What sort of place had they lived in before?

Flora came clomping up the stairs with more bedding in her arms. Michael laid the mattress down on a bed base and saw that straw spilt out of a hole. He brushed it nervously and more straw spilt down onto the floor.

"Ah, leave it," Flora told him. "Ma will re-stuff them all when she gets time."

The next loads were wooden shuttles with strands of rough creamy thread wound round them. "Up to the weaving room," Jethro told them.

The rhythmic clack of wood on wood could be heard as they staggered up the stairs to the second floor. Michael was not prepared for the shock that he felt as he stepped out into the weaving room. It was huge, and full of looms and weavers. Michael turned his head this way and that; up here there seemed to be no division between the houses. The top floor stretched away right up to the top of the street. The roof beams echoed to the low murmur of voices as men and boys worked away, and again, not an inch of space was left spare. Some of the weavers looked up from their work and waved, but they didn't stop, not for a moment.

George also stared, amazed at the sight. "Well, I'll be damned!" he chuckled. "I could march right up to the top o' the street and go downstairs an' eat someone else's dinner."

Just at that moment Jethro shouted up the stairs. "Ma's made porridge! Tell our lodger to come and sup!"

Chapter 7

Mouldy Bread

· ·

Down in the kitchen a good fire was burning
in the stove and Ma was spooning steaming
porridge into bowls, making Michael realize
that he was very hungry. He was made to sit
at the table in the seat of honour along with
Jethro, while the other children perched on
stools or crouched on the floor. It was only
then that Michael got a chance to count
them: three boys and six girls – what a
houseful!

The porridge was slightly salty with a
rather gritty texture to it, but despite that,
it was warm and filling and Michael ate
politely while at the back of his mind he
still panicked. How was he ever going to get
home again?

"Eat up, lads! Eat up!" Ma fussed. "The
bell will be ringing soon and you mustn't be

late, not for your first night's work. If one of us offends Mr Arkwright then we all do, and this fine home will be lost to us. They say he's very strict about it."

There seemed little need to hurry the three boys, for they all gobbled away at their food. Then suddenly the smallest boy got up, pale-faced and trembling.

"Look out, Ma, our Ben's going to be sick again," Flora cried.

Ben clamped his hand over his mouth and tried to make it to the back door, but was sick down the steps. Ma was up at once and wringing out a cloth in a wooden bucket to wipe his face. "Don't start this. Don't you dare start this, my lad!" she cried. "Not on the first day! We can't have George and Jack going off without you."

"I saw him!" Flora pointed mercilessly at Ben, who hardly seemed able to stand, so violently was he trembling. "I saw him steal mouldy bread from the rubbish tip at the inn, where we watered the pony."

"I saw him too." George shook his head.

Jethro was scratching his head and looking worried. "Eh, lad, we've told thee again and again tha mustn't eat mouldy bread no matter how hungry. We knew there'd be food once we got ourselves taken on here at Cromford."

Ben was in tears, but he clapped his hand to his mouth again. His mother grabbed him and rushed him outside. There was a worried silence for a moment; then a bell started ringing clearly in the distance.

"That's the bell for night shift!" Flora cried. "If only they'd let lasses go at night, then I'd go in Ben's place!"

George and Jack both got up and started pulling on their jackets.

Michael couldn't believe that a lad as young as Ben should be expected to go to work at night, and especially if he was sick. Jack was small enough and Ben even younger. But Michael knew what he'd seen on that advertisement: children of seven years and over.

Ma reappeared, dragging the white-faced Ben after her. "He's going to have to go," she insisted. "We can't let Mr Arkwright down on our first day, it'll ruin everything."

Michael was suddenly on his feet. He couldn't believe what he was saying, but the thought of little Ben struggling to work in the state he was in was just too dreadful. "I'll go in his place," he said. "If that'll be all right."

They all looked up at him uncertainly.

"Tha's too fine a lad to work in't mill," Ma whispered.

"I could do it just for tonight," Michael begged.

Then suddenly Flora was kissing him. "Bless you!" she said. "You'll save our bacon!"

"There's no time to lose." George was wrapping a ragged scarf about his neck and following Jack to the door.

"You can't go in those fine clothes of yours," Ma said. "Flora, bring down George's Sunday best."

*　　*　　*

Within minutes Michael was hurrying down
the hill towards Cromford market-place,
wearing rough, itchy trousers that finished
just below his knees, an off-white cotton shirt
with the sleeves rolled up and a rather tight
jacket and waistcoat. Though George was
about the same height, he was clearly a lot
thinner than Michael. Rough wooden clogs
slipped uncomfortably on his feet as slushy
snow slopped up the back of his legs. He'd
insisted on keeping his socks on and just
hoped nobody would notice them being
different. George and Jack urged him on
while the bell was still clanging, the sound
growing louder at every step.

Michael stumbled. "No streetlights," he
muttered. One or two of the other lads
carried flickering lanterns, but they gave out
little light. "Watch the cobbles! Mind the mill
leat!" George hissed.

They must have been somewhere near the
market-place, but Michael could see no sign

of the solid Greyhound Hotel with its huge clock. All there seemed to be was the rushing sound of water, gallons of it, running fast towards the mill in deep-cut channels.

They were not the only ones who were heading downhill, for out of the houses and cottages poured a great number of other young workers. They all jogged down the cobbled streets, shouting and jostling each other, some chewing at hunks of bread as they went. There was just no time for Michael to think about what he was doing. He looked up ahead and gasped, for as they rounded the bend in the cart track, two huge buildings came into view. The outlines were black in the darkness, but rows of windows blazed with yellow, flickering lights.

Chapter 8

Two Scavengers
and a Piecer

"There's two mills?" Michael gasped. He was sure that he'd never seen two mills down Mill Lane. "It's like New York!"

"New York? I've not been there," George told him, doubtfully.

"Nor me," Michael told him. "But ... I think it's got tall square buildings a bit like these."

A restless crowd had gathered at the main gates now, and as the boys joined it, the bell stopped ringing and the gates were swung wide open so that the workers could march inside.

"Where do we go?" Their pace slowed down a little and Michael had time to feel anxious.

"We've to report to the overseer," George told him. "Come along, Jack."

Young Jack was white-faced, but he strode ahead obediently. Seeing the small boy follow his brother so bravely made Michael determined too.

They were sent to wait outside the manager's office. The overseer came and took their names. Michael hesitated for a moment but George spoke for him. "This is our lodger, standing in for my brother, Benjamin Barraclough, who's sick."

"Aye," the overseer agreed. "Age?"

"I'm nine."

"Big lad for nine," the overseer said. "Big lad for a scavenger. I hope tha can bend and bow. Now then, George Barraclough, eleven years old, you can start straight in with the piecing! All go together to the seventh floor, second mill. Don't hang about! Time is money!"

They were striding fast across the open yard before they knew it. Michael thought it seemed a bit like being in the army. The overseer was like a sergeant-major barking orders and everyone had to obey. The main gates were being locked up behind them now that all the workers had arrived. No sneaking off in the middle of your work. Perhaps it was more like prison than the army.

Then suddenly a great creaking sound started up and with a whoosh the waterwheel beside the first mill started turning. Water flooded through deep-cut channels towards the second mill, where two more wheels groaned into action. It was a strange and terrifying place, this mill.

Michael glanced up at the great stone block of the second mill building. It stood seven storeys high, every window ablaze with candles and lamps.

George and Jack stared just as he did. "Eeh, I've never seen owt like this before," George muttered.

Jack said nothing, but his eyes were wide.

"Haven't you worked in a mill before?" Michael asked.

"Course not." George looked surprised at his question. "Great mills like this is a brand new thing. There's many as think they're wicked places, taking away poor home spinners' jobs. That's what Ma and Flora used to do."

"Then why have you come here?" Michael asked.

He shook his head. "Home workers just can't make a living any more. Ma and the lasses couldn't keep Father supplied with enough thread, no matter how hard they worked, and all we seemed to get was debts."

Michael nodded; he understood well enough how that could happen.

"Then we heard about Mr Arkwright's advertisement, and how he was offering fine houses for weavers' families."

"Was your house in Derby smaller?" Michael asked.

"Smaller? It were one room for us all," George laughed. Then he dropped his voice. "We shared it with another family, and pigs and chickens lodged beneath us, but though we lived in a hovel, at least Father were his own master. Now he must call Mr Arkwright 'master' and bow to his strict rules. They all swear that you sell your soul to Arkwright when you come here. Say nowt about it inside!"

They walked into the building and were sharply directed upstairs by another overseer. "Get on – no time to waste. The machines are running. Mr Jones will tell you what to do."

They strode up the stone stairway, passing floor after floor, plain whitewashed walls on either side of them, and on the seventh landing they came out into a huge barn-like room, filled with the thrum and clank of heavy wooden machines. Two huge drive shafts stretched the whole length of the ceiling, turning steadily. The workers, moving to and fro beneath them, looked like ants in among all the giant machinery and they all seemed to be suffering from bad coughs.

All three boys stared for a moment.

"I don't like it," Jack whispered. "What if those big works come toppling down upon us?"

"Nay," George whispered, taking his brother by the hand. "Look at all these folk working away underneath it all. You'll be safe." But Michael saw that George's own brows still met in a worried frown.

Down from the drive shafts came long leather belts that linked up with the whirring spinning-frames beneath, keeping them constantly moving.

"Don't stand gawping," a man bellowed, pointing at them. "Get up here and take thy place, there's no room for slackers on my floor."

All three moved fast towards him.

"Right now," he said. "Two scavengers and a piecer – that's what I'm told to expect."

George was sent to a row of machines further up.

"Tha's big for a scavenger, lad," the overseer told Michael. "Now then, it's thy job to pick up every scrap o' raw cotton that falls from the spinning-frames and every time the clock strikes the hour tha gets hold o' that broom and sweeps down the full length of the floor beneath your frames. This row of frames is yours," he told Jack. "And this un's thine," he showed Michael. "I want this floor kept spick and span, for if a scrap o' fluff should go floating towards a candle and set up a fire, Mr Arkwright will hold me responsible and there'll be hell to pay. But where will I be placing the blame?" The man bent down towards Michael and Jack, putting his red face unpleasantly close. "I say, where will I place the blame?"

"With us," Michael whispered, suddenly adding "sir" as an afterthought. He wanted desperately to protect Jack. What was his mother thinking of, sending him out to work like this when he really ought to be tucked up in his bed safe and sound? And how would young Ben cope when he came to work here?

Chapter 9

Night Shift

· ·

"What's tha waiting for? Get to it," the
overseer ordered.

They rushed to their row of machines.

At first Michael was relieved at the
simplicity of the work, but it wasn't long
before he realized that Jack did have an
advantage. Creeping under the whirring
machinery was easier if you were small; it
wasn't long before every muscle in his body
was aching, so that it was almost a relief
when the floor manager called out "Sweep!"
and he could get up off his hands and knees
and run to get the broom. There was a smelly
toilet, hidden behind a curtain, right next to
all the work – no excuse to sneak away, even
for that!

There was no chance to speak to George,
and it would have been hard to hear what he

said against the constant noise of the machinery. At least Michael could see him on the next row of frames, side-stepping constantly up and down the row, catching the bits of thread that had broken, carefully fastening them as quickly as he could. Another older lad called John Thompson walked back and forth, setting full bobbins of chunky, roughly twisted cotton roving at the top of the machine, and taking away the lower bobbins when they were full of spun cotton thread. Michael saw that every now and again John Thompson pushed a small skein of cotton thread deep into his trouser pockets.

Michael paused for a moment to watch him. "What's tha gawping at?" John Thompson asked.

"Nothing." Michael got quickly on with his sweeping again. What he was interested in was the row of bobbins that turned steadily at the bottom of each frame. They slowly filled up with creamy-coloured thread and seemed to be exactly like his bobbin; the one that had brought him here and then so worryingly vanished. It was all crazy, but he couldn't help wondering if one of these bobbins could be his special one. Maybe if he could find the right one, it would take him home again. But there were hundreds of them! It seemed a mad idea, but no other plan would come to mind. Somehow he had to get back to his parents and away from this terrible place.

The hours passed by and Michael's back began to ache badly. A clock at the other end of the great noisy room struck the hour. At last the clock struck eleven and Michael felt sure that they must be due to finish soon. They couldn't expect young lads to work after midnight, could they? He was hungry and exhausted when at last a smaller bell inside the building rang.

"Are we finished?" Jack asked.

A cackle of laughter burst from John Thompson. He didn't even try to speak, but shook his head and put his hand to his mouth, then patted his belly. They quickly understood what he meant – they were going to have a food break. Thank goodness for that, thought Michael.

The overseer came down to the end of the room. "Scavengers' and spinners' dinner," he told them. He sent John Thompson along with them and told George to watch his machines while he was away.

Michael and Jack followed the older boy back down the stairs and into another whitewashed room with tables and two wood-burning stoves. Michael didn't know what to expect – perhaps a simple sort of canteen – but what he found cheered him enormously. There were Ma and Flora ladling hot soup into three bowls.

There was no time to relax. "Get eating quick and back to work!" a fat woman ordered. She seemed to be in charge of the dinner room.

Ma was full of whispered thanks to Michael. "Our Ben has stopped his sickness and he's fast asleep," she murmured. "I can't thank you enough. I really can't."

Her gratitude revived him as much as the soup. It was simply boiled-up vegetables with a few oats sprinkled in, but it was warm and filling. They ate it with some little chewy pancakes that Ma called oatcakes. Oats seemed to be everywhere; Michael wondered if he'd ever be able to face porridge again.

"Bobbins, water and oats," he muttered.

All too soon they were scraping their bowls clean and being hurried back upstairs. "How much longer do we work?" he asked as they reached the seventh floor.

John Thompson looked surprised and held up his hands to show six fingers.

"What, six in the morning? We work all night?"

John nodded. For a moment Michael felt like walking straight out of the building, but then he remembered the clang of the big gates as they'd closed behind him, and the turn of the key in the lock. They must have opened the gates again to let Ma and Flora in with the food. Could he slip out with them? But then he'd have no chance to try and find his bobbin.

George was sent to get his dinner as soon as they got back. The clock struck one and the overseer cried "Sweep!" Then a whispered message was passed from worker to worker.

"He's watching ... from Rock House!"

"Mr Arkwright's at his window!"

"No slacking!"

"Work fast!"

Michael glanced out of the window nearest to him. All was darkness around the mill except for one distant window showing light up on the hillside. The silhouette of a stout man could be seen against an oil-lamp's glow.

"He'll see thee looking," John Thompson hissed, "and then we'll all be for it!"

Michael stooped again to his work. Did the man never sleep? Did he stand there watching his mills all night long?

As the hours passed Michael became more

aware than ever of the striking of the clock. Every time it happened John held up the number of fingers of the hour. One, two and three o'clock passed slowly in a terrible, aching dream. Michael's back and shoulders had gone numb and he began to cough as the cotton fluff got up his nose and down his throat. At last John Thompson held up five fingers and grinned; his thumb jerked upwards and Michael realized with relief that there was only one hour left. His ordeal was nearly over, but then he remembered sadly that little Jack and Ben would be here every night until they grew big enough to be piecers. And though he was desperate for the shift to finish, Michael still hadn't found his special bobbin. He couldn't get rid of the idea that if he were ever to find it again, this was where he must look.

Suddenly the machinery seemed to be slowing down; gears were shifted and the vast workplace quietened a bit.

"Last sweep up!" the overseer roared.

Chapter 10

A Bit of Firewood

The great belts stopped and even the huge drive shafts above their heads stopped turning. Michael was so weary that he could scarcely think straight. "Must get out of here," he muttered. "Bobbin or not, I must get out!"

Then as he walked past the end of the row of spinning-frames he saw some of the older lads dipping into a basket of cracked bobbins and walking out with them tucked under their arms. His heart started beating wildly when he bent down to look and thought that he saw it – his own special bobbin – the crack exactly the same. He dived down to snatch it, his heart thundering like a drum and beads of sweat breaking out on his forehead. He mustn't be parted from it now.

"Hey, watch it, there's plenty for all," John

Thompson told him.

"Can we take them?"

"Oh aye, they're no good for spinning once they're cracked. We take 'em home to carve or for firewood. Mr Arkwright allows it."

"I should think he does," Michael muttered, clinging tightly to the bobbin, feeling that his whole life depended on it.

Then as he followed John Thompson out of the mill, the overseer and another man swooped down on them and grabbed the older boy. "Let me be!" John yelled.

Michael clutched his bobbin, trembling with fright at the sudden movement and fierce shouting voices.

"Let me be!" John howled. But the men ignored him and held him tightly, digging their hands down into his pockets, bringing out the skeins of creamy cotton that Michael had seen him hiding away.

"Tha knows the penalty for stealing cotton," the overseer growled. "Seven days in the lock-up, or you and your mother shall be turned from your home. I've had my eye on thee for a while, my lad!"

"Give us a chance, mister," John begged. He'd stopped struggling now and his voice turned soft and pleading. "Please give us another chance, mister?"

"Not worth my job," the overseer growled.

Then John was dragged away between the two men while Michael searched frantically for Jack and George.

They met up at last in the mill yard and set off fast together, heading past braying donkeys loaded with heavy baggage, towards the now open gates. The waterwheels in their deep cuts were still and silent. The workers left quietly, too weary to speak.

They'd almost reached the top of the hill when they passed a stone building, where they heard more raised voices and angry shouts. They looked towards it fearfully. "Lock-up!" George told him. "That's where they're taking John Thompson."

"Like a prison?" Michael asked.

"Aye. 'Tis a prison," George told him. "If tha breaks any one o' Mr Arkwright's rules tha'll be locked up there for days, and mostly in the dark. I heard them talking about it, it's a terrible place. They'll put thee in there for drunkenness or even being late for work!"

Michael strode on up the hill, shuddering and clinging tightly to his precious bobbin. "Got to get home! Got to get home!" he chanted under his breath.

When at last they arrived back at the house in North Street, the light from the lantern that Ma held high fell on his bobbin. He turned it quickly upside down. Where were the letters FL? His heart thundered again in panic. Was this his bobbin or not? The crack was right, but where were the carved letters? If it wasn't his special one, then he might never manage to get away from this harsh place.

"What's this?" Ma asked.

"Firewood," George told her. "We can bring them every day."

"That's grand," she said. "Put them down by the hearth and sit and eat."

"This one's mine!" Michael insisted.

"Of course it is," Ma soothed. "Put it down by the hearth, it'll be safe there while tha sups."

Michael was so hungry that he did as she said and tucked into his bowl of porridge. When at last he'd taken the edge off his hunger, he glanced over to the hearth and saw with horror that Flora was sitting there hacking away at his special bobbin with a small sharp knife. He leapt up from his stool, ready to shout at her – but then he stopped. He couldn't believe it. She'd cut into the wood the two letters that were so familiar to him – FL, sloping slightly outwards, just as they'd always done. He understood now. They weren't somebody's initials at all – they never had been. They were the beginning of Flora's name.

She looked up at him, her forehead wrinkled in frustration. "I always forget," she muttered. "Flora, Flora, F … L … and what is it that makes 'ora'?"

Michael crouched down beside her, calm now. He took up another cracked bobbin. "Let me show you," he said.

Flora willingly handed him the knife and he set to work at once. With all the family gathered about him he hacked away until at last he'd neatly made the whole name, FLORA, each letter well spaced, around the circular un-cracked bottom of the bobbin.

"Oh, look at that, Ma – my whole name all beautifully spelt out!" Flora took it and held it up for her mother to see.

Michael smiled at the pleasure such a simple thing had given. But then Flora picked up the other bobbin, his special bobbin, and grabbed the knife from his hand. "Now I know what comes next," she said, "I can carve my whole name."

"No!" Michael yelled. He just knew that mustn't happen and snatched the bobbin from her. "I must keep it."

"But I can make it better now!" Flora tried to grab it back.

"I like it just the way it is," he said.

"Let him be, Flora," Ma spoke sharply.

Flora looked at him curiously again. "Tha's a funny lad," she said. Then before he knew what she was up to, she kissed him on the cheek again.

Michael felt himself blushing bright red. He wasn't used to girls doing that to him, but at least she'd let him have the bobbin back.

"Come on now, lads," Ma said. "You get yourselves off to bed."

"I've got to go," Michael told them. "I've got to go and I might be away a long time. Don't worry about me, I'll be fine. And I must take this bobbin with me."

Chapter 11

You Can't Stop Progress

They looked a little puzzled, but they let him change his clothes and go outside into the snowy street once again. He stood there on North Street in the half-light of morning feeling sorry to be leaving them, but there was no doubt about it – he had to get back to the twenty-first century. He looked hopefully at the bobbin. "Well," he said, "go on, do it again. Spin me through time! I've got to go home!"

The bobbin just lay there quiet and still.

"Oh *please!* What did I do?" he fretted. Then he remembered and started tipping his hand so that the bobbin rolled back and forth. "Oh yes," he whispered, "that's it. Please take me home!"

The bobbin started rolling wildly, and at last it seemed to be moving of its own accord.

Michael took a deep breath and grabbed it tightly round the middle with both hands. When he felt the lurch that sent him spinning, he was glad. It was unpleasant but he knew that it was right. He shut his eyes as he spun, trying to make the whole thing less scary.

At last he sensed that he was slowing down and dared to open them again. Yes, there was North Street just gently tipping about him, and there was his school at the top of the street. He was standing at his own front door, familiar red curtains hanging up at the window.

"Are you all right?" Sarah was still in front of her door, watching him with a frown on her face. "You look a bit dizzy – I thought you were going to fall over!"

"Yes, thank you," he said, smiling. "I'm absolutely fine."

"See you in the morning, then," she said, with a friendly wave and a smile that somehow reminded him of Flora.

He went into his own house and met his mother coming down the stairs looking glum. "Hi, sweetheart," she sighed.

"What's wrong?" he asked.

"Oh," his mother shrugged her shoulders. "I'm probably being impatient but we've had that website up and running for a week now and we haven't even had an e-mail, never mind an order. I don't know whether this is going to work. Perhaps it was a stupid idea!"

Michael was filled with relief to be back home with his parents, in his own time and place. "It was a great idea," he told her. "You've got to move with the times. You can't fight progress!"

His mother smiled and dropped a kiss on his head. "You've come home in a very good mood," she said.

"Yes," he nodded. "And it really does feel like home."

Michael went off to school eagerly in the morning. Mr Price began talking to them about Sir Richard Arkwright and his mills; how there was little left now of the great second mill.

"The one that was seven storeys high?" Michael butted in.

Mr Price didn't mind at all. "Glad you've been studying this, Michael," he said. "Tell us what else you've been finding out about the mills."

Michael shook his head. Where could he start?

After school that day Sarah walked homewards down North Street beside him. "My grandma used to live in your house," she told him, "when she was a little girl."

"Did she?" he was suddenly interested.

"Yes," said Sarah. "My family lived in your house for years and years and they all worked in the mills."

Michael stopped and stared at her. No wonder her smile had reminded him of Flora – she might be Flora's great-great-granddaughter or something like it. He couldn't think what on earth to say, but he found the idea quite comforting. Perhaps he hadn't lost Flora and her family after all.

When they reached his own doorway his mother knocked excitedly on the attic window at him and stuck out her head. "We've got an e-mail from Japan!" she cried. "A Japanese clothing firm is sending one of their buyers to see us. They like the look of our designs."

"Heavens!" Sarah whispered, clearly impressed.

Nothing could surprise Michael now. "See," he yelled, "I knew it would work!"

Michael was about to open his front door when Sarah stopped beside him. "Do you want to come to my house?" she asked. "I've got something to show you."

Michael felt pleased by the invitation. "OK," he grinned.

Sarah's house was laid out in exactly the same pattern as Michael's. She led him into the living-room and pointed out a fancy, patterned bobbin on the mantelpiece. Someone had covered it in carefully painted flowers, just a little worn with age.

"There," she said. "This is the bobbin I told you about. I wouldn't take that to school."

Michael smiled politely, but as he looked closely his heart began to thump. There, cut into one end of the bobbin, were the familiar letters, FLORA. Michael's hands shot out to pick it up, but then he hesitated.

"May I?" he asked.

"Course you can, if you're careful," Sarah smiled.

Michael's hands were trembling as he held it close to his face. There was no doubt about it – this was the bobbin that he'd carved for Flora. It had had a lot of other decoration added to it, but the letters cut into the top were definitely his very own handiwork.

Sarah watched him, satisfied with the expression of amazement on his face.

"Grandma told us that it had been passed

down through our family for generations and she said that we must always keep it. The person who cut the letters was someone who helped the family, just when they really needed it."

"And they've kept it all these years." Michael could hardly believe it.

"I somehow thought you'd like it!"

"Oh yes," said Michael, carefully replacing it on the mantelpiece. "You were quite right. I like it very, very much."